Two Suns

Kris Solo

Published by Kris Solo, 2024.

TWO SUNS

First edition. February 22, 2024.

ISBN: 979-8224687893

Written by Kris Solo.

Table of Contents

From The Author

I had a dream once. It was an incredibly bright colored dream. The feeling was so vivid that when I woke up, I could not understand where the reality was.

Many dreams come true to one degree or another. Since then, I've been recording the most unusual dreams and using them in my stories.

This story is not only a description of my dream or vision, but also the fruit of my imagination. The distant stars, planets and space in general attract and will attract people to itselves. People have always sought the unattainable. In the near future colonization of the planets will become routine and necessary. But wherever a person walks, he will destroy everything around. People will have to face the inhabitants of these planets. And to survive, they will need to make a decision: to be in harmony with the local people or destroy. It is important for people to understand that harmony with the inhabitants of another planet is a more correct decision. But will it be so?

In the fantastic story "Two Suns" it is said about the people who destroyed the native planet, about the fight, with himself, with hostile creatures-the conquerors and the spiritual agreement with the nativecivilians alien of the planet. In the description of the heroes, the deep double meaning of the inner world of man is hidden. Different personalities of heroes make up a whole personality: a destructive person, a conquering person and a man-rescuer. Even the heroes – Darguns and Moruki - from a person a lot.

I gave each character a part of my character, divided my inner world. After reading this story, you can learn from some hero. Perhaps you will learn something and make the appropriate conclusions for yourself. Are you and your next generation ready for this possible future? Maybe we should start preparing?

July Of The 2026 Year. Somewhere On The Earth.

The catastrophically rapid warming of the climate on the whole planet has led to complete confusion among people and a lack of understanding of what is happening. Scientists around the world have discovered more than twelve livable planets, but which is the worst, the appearance of a comet was expected. The presence of an uninvited visitor - a comet - did not bode well for the further life of the inhabitants of the Earth.

There are places on the blue planet where not everyone can reach. The only road to one of these places is through the impassable jungle. Over the past decades, the nature of the Earth has radically changed. Plants changed and began to resemble the flora of Africa, the place of Ruwenzori, and Australia. The fauna has changed not only due to natural phenomena, but also the "activity" of human minds and hands. And now, in the midst of these jungle animals are walking - mutants, including dinosaurs and nobody knows from where they appeared.

So, only the old man Stanley knows about this road, who carries the groceries in the cart from the nearest village. Residents of this village, too, know about this road, but they do not go there, since this place is not particularly attractive in any way. Why? Because it's a monastery. The female monastery. Here and now the old Stanley is carrying food... and two monks.

"And why did they send us to another monastery?" Sighed Johnny.

"Attacks on this monastery have recently become more frequent," the old man said. "So they needed security."

"Well, and we, then what does this have to do with it?" Nestor was surprised. The old man, only, shrugged his shoulders. Two twenty-nine-year-old guys have been in the monastery for three years already. Before a quiet peaceful life they were bullies, loved girls, and went on motorcycles. In general, they were tough guys. What motivated them to go to the monastery, they themselves do not know. Johnny and Nestor were obedient monks. Parents were shocked by the act of their adult children, but eventually got used to and calmed down. "God," whispered Johnny, when they saw a mesmerizing picture. Before them appeared a monastery, grown into a steep rock. The fence of the monastery was high, made of solid black wood. But such a fence did not stop the attackers. A mighty forest towered around the monastery.

The old man went to the huge gate and knocked. The gate opened, and the old man struck the reins along the sides of the horse. In the yard they were waiting for Sister Maria.

"You to her," said the old man and led the horse further. The monks jumped off the cart and approached the nun.

"Please follow me," said Sister Maria and led the guests to abbess.

They walked along a stone path, which amusingly wriggling in different directions. Sequoiaudendrons about a hundred meters high, palm trees trachicarpus, American palm trees Washington, eucalyptus and many other plants rose along its sides. On the right a small pond also was buried in greenery.

· · · ·

"DAMN IT!" JOHNNY EXCLAIMED when he saw the nuns hiding behind trees and bushes.

They looked and smiled. Sister Mary entered the monastery and for a long time led the young monks along the corridors. Stopping near the painted door, she asked the monks to wait outside the door and went into the office. A minute later, Johnny and Nestor were already standing in front of the mother - abbess.

"So," Fatigue flashed across her face. "Where did you come from?"

"Here are the documents," Johnny handed a folder with papers to the mother - abbess, "and recommendations."

"So," wailed the strict woman, looking through the documents. She putt folder a side and left the table.

"So. You were sent here to guard the monastery and its territory. The fact is that local men and travelers began to penetrate here," the woman walked from corner to corner, holding his hands behind his back. "We have a female monastery. And in the last three months, five nuns were raped. In addition, two of them were torn to pieces by predators."

"But why did not you hire special guards?" Nestor asked.

"Because it's a monastery." The abbess answered. "And you are monks. Do you understand me?"

"Yes," answered Johnny and Nestor.

"Let's go. I'll show you your house."

The abbess took them out of the monastery and showed a small house where the monks will live. This house was located in the monastery near the main gate.

"Here you will live. It has two separate rooms and a kitchen. Sister Catalina will bring you food. You are not allowed to enter the monastery, unless I call you. I'll tell her to bring line," said the abbess and walked away majestically.

The monks entered the house and examined the rooms: each contained a wooden bed, a table, a chair, the image of the Saints in front of a small altar for prayers. They distributed the rooms among themselves, sat down at the table in the kitchen. There was a knock at the door.

"Come in," the monks said at the same time, but no one came in. The knock repeated. Johnny looked at Nestor, got up from the table and, opening the door, looked out. Behind the door stood a young blue eyed nun, about seventeen.

"Who are you?" Johnny asked awkwardly.

"Nun," she looked at the monk in surprise.

"I see. What is your name?"

"Catalina. Sister Catalina." She held a stack of bed linen in her hands.

"Did you bring linen?"

"Aha," her big eyes sparkled with naughtiness. She had never seen such a funny monk as she thought. "Mattresses under the beds."

He nodded and took the bed linens from her velvety gentle hands.

"Mother Theresa..."

"Theresa?" Asked the monk, who was about to go into the house.

"The abbess of the monastery," Sister Catalina explained. "So, she asked to convey that the service we have is in the church. You can come."

She handed in a piece of paper with a schedule of prayer services and feeding.

"The dinner will be at seven in the evening."

Johnny he looked at the leaving figure of the nun. Turning the schedule in his hands, he entered the house.

"Well, who was there?" Nestor asked.

"Lord," Johnny replied, putting a piece of paper on the table.

"Very funny." Nestor looked at the schedule.

"They are crazy. At six in the morning for a prayer," Johnny grumbled.

"Be careful. You're a monk." Nestor took the bed linen and went to his room. Johnny withdrew to his room. Covering the bed, he fell to the bed and exclaimed,

"My God!"

Nestor appeared in the doorway:

"Why are you yelling?"

"Just imagine, Nestor! There are only nuns around!"

"And you are a monk. And do not forget about it."

"Why did you spoil my mood?" Johnny growled. Nestor smiled and went into the kitchen.

"Yes, I am a monk," Johnny said and followed. "But I'm a man too!"

"Johnny, a monk is no longer a man." Nestor sat down at the table. "Let's decide how we will guard such a large territory of the monastery."

Johnny sat opposite Nestor. They decided that they would do a circumvention of the territory every half hour. Then the monks went in search of the church. Judging by the bell tower, she was right behind the monastery. Entering the church, the monks felt a lot of curious eyes. The service began, but the secret peeping of the nuns around them continued until the end. After the service, the monks went to their dwelling and sat down to supper (probably sister Catalina brought dinner while they looked around the neighborhood of the monastery).

Ominous blood-red moon ruled over darkness. It was complete and extraordinarily huge. There was a feeling that if you reach out, you can touch it. This night it was very quiet, so quiet that it became creepy.

"It's strange. Night birds do not sing, crickets do not chirp…" Johnny said. "Even bats do not fly."

"Like before the storm," Nestor nodded. The monks made another round.

· · · ·

"DAPHNE!" SOMEONE CALLED the girl walking along the street.

"Daphne!" It was repeated. The girl turned and smiled. She was approached by a tall guy.

"Hey, Spike."

"Daphne, did you hear about the comet?"

"Yes," the girl from time to time looked at people going from the store. "They say that a collision with the Earth is inevitable."

"We'll die if that happens," Spike said with hope for life. "I wonder when she will appear?"

Daphne looked at the sky.

"There she is," the girl said quietly. The guy slowly raised his eyes. The sun on this day was unusually bright, but it did not stop Spike to see tail of a fireball. The weather began to deteriorate and people saw something in the sky and hurried home. There came a breeze which began to intensify. The sun has faded. The dogs disappeared somewhere.

"What is it?" Asked Spike.

"Comet..."

Instead of a comet, there was now a turquoise stain that sprawled across the sky.

"I think it exploded," the girl suggested. "Or it collided with something."

"In my opinion, both that, and another."

"In any case, it's time for us to run, because it will rain on us." And they ran across the road to the house. A dirty turquoise rain in front of them. Daphne shouted to Spike that it was impossible to get under this rain, since he was probably poisonous and could kill them. They ran to the left, trying to round the rain, but there it blocked the way for people. Then they ran in the rain, at random. Running into the house, the girl and the guy climbed the stairs to the attic room. There were people waiting for them already. There they were already waiting. In this house lived a woman with three children, her two sisters and brother. For some reason, it was necessary to be saved in the attic. Why, no one knew, but knew that the higher, the safer. So spoke the inner voice.

"Hello everyone," the girl chirped cheerfully.

"Hi."

"Oh. I got soaked through." Daphne took the towel that brought Eddie and went into the attic shower. "Spike something else is not right, but I'm all up to the thread. Ah, if I will die, so I shall die."

"It's not rain, it's some kind of porridge," complained Spike. "As if lying in the mud."

"Yeah," the woman who breast-fed the baby chuckled. "You are lying in the mud like a pig."

"Do not mock me, Dorothy."

After Daphne emerged from the shower, smelling pure, Spike immediately went to wash off the swinishness caused by an uninvited heavenly body.

It was dark outside. The sky was occasionally lit by a strange lightning, pouring dirty turquoise rain. The window of the attic room was lit up by the light of the lightning, and it was clear how the seated people were watching the sky.

In their eyes, the horror of what was happening and the expectation of an unknown future were reflected. Daphne leaned out of the window. On the left appeared something resembling a ball lightning and painfully "stung" the girl in her outstretched left arm. The electric charge passed through along the arm to the elbow.

"Daphne, close the window," was heard Dorothy's frightened voice. The girl cursed and closed the window. The glowing ball with a silvery tinge immediately disappeared. Daphne sat down on the sofa, rubbing the elbow of her left hand.

"Here's the creature!" Indignantly exclaimed the girl.

• • • •

IN THE VICINITY OF the monastery there was a frenzied barking and howl of dogs which was heard from a nearby village and awakening not only the inhabitants of this same village, but also the inhabitants of the monastery. The foliage of trees, palm trees and bushes went swayed, because animals and birds screamed, roared, and raved. The inhabitants of the monastery were horrified. They did not understand what caused such a stir and were afraid, what frightened animals and dinosaurs will break the fence. The monks screamed with fear and ran back and forth. Johnny and Nestor did not know what to do.

The sun faded, but the darkness did not come. It was light, but the light was strange. Suddenly, there was a lull. And this silence was painfully long, as if time had stopped. Everyone was waiting for something. They stood and looked at the extinguished sun. It did not hurt the eyes. Suddenly, everyone was blinded by the unnaturally bright glow coming from behind, behind the backs of people.

The inhabitants of the monastery, covering their eyes with their hands, turned towards the source of light. The blue sun. People were amazed at the appearance of a new star with a bright blue glow. They turned their heads in the direction of the yellow sun - it was in place and did not go anywhere. They looked toward the new blue sun - and it's there. Two suns! Now on Earth two suns ruled the day.

Eight Years Later.

"Jesus," Johnny groaned, "we live like monkeys because of these lizards."

Nestor grinned. He sat on the floor of the hut, made arrows for the crossbow and watched the other.

"I cannot eat normally," continued Johnny, "to wash... And why the hell should I live on a tree?!"

"The Lord will cut off your tongue," Nestor smiled. "Sit down and calm down."

Johnny sat on his bed in a lotus position, took a banana from a round wooden table.

"There is not a single woman here. There were so many of them in the monastery!"

"Why not? There is."

"There is. Do you know how many kilometers to pass to meet at least one? And anyway, why did not we make the dwelling under the ground? And then you'll go out in the morning to the "balcony", and there is a pimply face of a fifteen-meter lizard before you there."

"Yeah. And if you lived under the ground, you would every day, only do that, digging your hole from the ground and manure of lizards."

"That's for sure," Nestor. "But here it is not safe either. Someday, our hut will be carried along with us by a running animal."

"It's not safe everywhere now."

After the celestial metamorphosis, the people of the whole planet had to leave their homes, as the monsters grew bolder and began to attack more often. Small colonies and single people arranged for themselves dwellings in tall trees, under the ground and in hollows of thick trees. Not many settled in caves of rocks. They had to abandon civilization and return to the primitive way of life. Only so they could survive.

People again began to make bows, arrows, spears, crossbows, again began to wear clothes from the skins of animals. Of course, many tried to keep at least something of civilization and so in their primitive dwellings there were beautiful modern beds, bed-linen, tables, armchairs, couches...

• • • •

THERE WERE ALSO SUCH people - they lived in small towns. Yes, the city remained. A high twenty-meter high steel fence was made around it. In addition, security is constantly working there, cameras are installed everywhere. In general, there was an ordinary life - people worked, had fun. Agriculture has developed in cities. Only in the cities it was possible. Vegetables and other products were sent by helicopters to Mount of Plenty. There are many places where food was goes. It is a help to people living in forests, who cannot maintain their garden. On the Mountain there is a cellar, in which food was stored until people have disassembled it. And so every months.

Of course, many people want to live in the city, but it is very difficult to live there. In the city strictly monitor the population. But not only food is brought to the Mountain of Abundance. In this cellar a forest people find clothes, shoes, various industrial goods, medicines, in general, everything that can be useful for life.

Life in the jungle is very difficult. If someone is sick or injured, then you are your own doctor. And if you are not your own doctor, you'll have to go to a real doctor who lives in a huge thick tree. Well, or at worst, into the city.

"Johnny, it's time for us."

Nestor fixed the purse belts with arrows, threw the crossbow on his shoulder.

"Nestor, it's too early," groaned the monk, lying on the hard bed.

"If we leave early, we'll be in time before dark. Get up."

Nestor lowered the staircase, made of ropes and sticks, and descended to the ground.

"Johnny, do not forget about the stairs."

"It is late," Johnny groaned.

Nestor looked at the monk who had fallen from the hut. They threw the ladder back and left only the rope, securing it by the tree. The dense thickets of the jungle aroused fear. Everywhere there was a danger that at any moment could show out all its power.

"And why do we live so far away from this mountain?"

"Rejoice, because others live even farther away," Nestor raised his palm up, letting Johnny stop to stop.

"What is it? The Ninja Turtle?" Whispered Johnny.

"No. A little harmless quick lizard.Ahead stood a five-meter young dinosaur."

He sniffed.

"What does she want?" Johnny whispered, peering over the Nestor's back.

"It wants to have for breakfast us. It noticed us."

The monks turned and ran into the depths of the jungle. The terrible roar of the t-Rex spread around the district. Pursuing the prey among the trees was difficult, so it went to the open area, abandoning this venture.

They fled, not looking back and maneuvering between the trees. At some point something happened. Understanding came only when Johnny opened his eyes. The clash was terrible, and, Johnny was furious. Under his body lay a girl with almost black eyes, her eyes also threw thunder and lightning. Nestor stood aside, leaning his back on the tree, and smiling.

"Could you get off me?" Daphne said indignantly.

"And, can we lie down?"

Daphne with force threw off a cheeky man, rose from the ground and disappeared behind the trees.

"Cutie," Johnny said, rising from the ground and looking at the figure of the girl disappearing in the thickets.

"Oh!" cried Johnny. The Mountain of Abundance was like an anthill: people were crouching like ants.

"So we'll stay here until the morning."

People went down one by one to the basement, but among the peaceful crowd there were always intruders. And now a man pushed a woman with a little girl of eight. Daphne ran to the rough man and punched him in the jaw. He fell to the ground.

"Are you okay?" She asked the woman.

"Yes."

"And your girl?"

"Yes, thank you."

"Here's your cutie," Nestor said. The monks approached the people and stood in line. After several hours, Johnny grumbled

Disappointedly,

"Do we really have to go back?"

Nestor only looked at his friend without a word in response. They sat on the ground waiting for their turn. People murmured against each other, cursing everything in the world. The dinosaur's rumbling, which rang out all over the district like a thunderclap, made people silent. A minute later they were already hiding wherever. The crackling of broken trees and bushes announced the approach of a hunter - a tyrannosaurus. True, these animals now did not look exactly the same as they used to be.

The monks exchanged glances and ran to the cellar. In a panic, the basement remained open, and the monks decided to take advantage of the opportunity. They went down and closed the lid. It was heard how people were running above them and how the dinosaur was running after them. How long it would last, the monks did not know, so they risked freezing in this basement.

"Okay, let's see what we have here," Nestor said. The monks took everything they needed and put them in bags. They took exactly as much as they could carry, but in order to survive at least a week or two. Behind them there was a noise, and the monks turned.

"Hello," the voice belonged to the same girl Johnny faced.

"Hey. What are you doing here?" Johnny asked, not without interest.

"The same as you," Daphne answered, and continued to fill her bag.

"These lizards are definitely hampering our existence," growled Johnny.

"All these creatures are God's creatures, like us," Nestor said in a tranquil voice.

"Besides, they are the true inhabitants of this planet."

"And we invaded their planet and destroyed them," the girl added, looking at the basement lid.

"It was a long time ago." Johnny was unhappy with the conversation. "And now..."

"And now they are destroying us," Daphne finished. She is clearly mocking me, Johnny thought evilly, but said aloud:

"Personally, I did not destroy them. The aliens arrived and they destroyed all of them. Then aliens settled us on this planet."

"For them we are aliens." Nestor raised his hand, forcing the monk and the girl to shut up. "It seems the dinosaur is gone. Quietly it became."

"Indeed, it's quiet." Johnny agreed. They slowly opened the basement lid and looked out. There was nobody around, only a few corpses lay here and there. People climbed out of the basement, closed the lid and parted.

It was almost dark when the monks approached their house on the tree. It was heard the sound of a flying helicopter. The beam of the searchlight hit the monks in the face when they looked up, then something painfully stuck into their bodies and their consciousness clouded. Waking up, the monks began to inspect the place where they were. Nestor looked at his right shoulder.

"Sung as animals."

The room in which they were, looked usually: a small, gently-blue walls, a table and two beds at the sides. A few minutes later the door opened and four people entered the room: two in black suits, two in military uniforms of khaki color and holding the same clothes in their hands.

"Where are we?" Nestor asked.

"You are in the city. Change clothes," said the man in black, probably the main one. They threw clothes on the beds.

"You will go with others outside the Solar System, master one of the planets," the chief continued.

"Can we refuse?" Nestor asked.

"No. You will be sent in any case, whether you like it or not."

"Follow us." He said that when the monks disguised themselves.

They walked along narrow corridors past different doors.

"Can you use your weapons?" The chief asked. There was no emotion in his voice that made the monks somehow uncomfortable.

"Ah... the crossbow will not help?" Johnny asked with hope.

"No."

The monk looked sympathetically at Nestor, foreseeing the worst.

"Training will begin today."

"Training?" The monks exchanged glances.

Within a month, they were trained along with other captured people in an accelerated mode: they fired from various types of firearms, threw hunting knives, climbed the ropes and rocks, conducted hand-to-hand combat, prepared for the flight.

The planet Tana.

How many people were on the ship, the monks did not know: they were put in capsules, and then loaded onto the ship. None of the passengers flying on the ship knew what planet they were being taken to and what the conditions for life were. All they knew was that the atmosphere on that planet was the same as on Earth. They "slept" as long as the ship's system did not turn off the capsules. People looked at each other. The total number of passengers was twenty, not counting the crew of the ship. Among the colonists was a girl already familiar to monks.

"Look." Said Nestor, elbowing his friend the monk. "The ways of the Lord are inscrutable."

"Yeah," Johnny sighed a little sadly. "Attention, - a voice came from the speakers. - The captain of this ship is speaking. I ask you to fasten your seat belts. We enter the atmosphere of the planet Tana." A few minutes later, the shaking began: the ship entered the atmosphere.

"Well, we've landed," said the dark-skinned big man. "All right, guys. I am your Lead. I'll take you to the base. Now we take five boxes with provisions in the cargo hold and unload. Clear? Then go ahead."

As soon as the colony of people came out, the ship climbed into the sky and flew away. A desert appeared before people. There were yellow sand and nothing more.

"It's wonderful," the bespectacled protested.

"So. Have all arranged in a line. Sergeant Parker, come to me. The host turned to the sergeant and said: Give everyone weapons."

The colonists walked, heavily moving their legs: the sand made it difficult for them to move. Half an hour later the sands ended, and before them the forest appeared.

"Be careful. Keep your weapons ready," the Leader warned. It was unusually hot, but the rays of the three suns almost did not penetrate thanks to the trees and bushes. The trees were quite tall, resembling moose horns. Their branches were covered with dense light-violet

16

foliage. Nestor lifted the sheet from the ground and examined it: the size of a little longer than a hand', a thin, elongated shape.

"Do not fall behind!" Shouted sergeant Parker. Nestor threw the leaf; it fell like a feather bird feather, swinging from side to side. Nature here was ominously beautiful. Above the heads there were various sounds, probably of some birds and animals, of insect chatter. A shout of a man was heard ahead of him. One of the bushes entangled a thin man by his "mustache" and dragged it to the open bud at the top of the main trunk. From there appeared two large plates with "teeth" like a sundew. Side branches with wide leaves about a meter in diameter embraced the man and began to push him inside of the bud. The man screamed and wriggled, trying to free himself. Others tried to help him, but the Leader stopped them:

"Do not shoot! You will not help him, already, do not help."

The cry died down, a crunch of broken bones was heard.

"Remember this plant. And do not go near it."

"What the hell is this?" The bespectacled asked by a quivering voice. "Where did you bring us?"

He was on the verge of collapse, his hands were trembling, which caused the revolver to fall and shoot.

"Damn it, calm down!" The Leader picked up the fallen revolver and put it back into the hand of the bespectacled.

"Sergeant," the Leader said, "takes this idiot under the scope. If he does something stupid again, shoot him."

Four-eyes bulged. Others became indignant.

"Quiet!" The Leader cried. "We'll shoot them all."

After an hour and a half, the Leader led the colonists to a glade where the base was located. It was evident that it was abandoned. At least, people were not visible.

"What happened here?" Asked the dark-skinned man. "Where are all people gone? It's a human base, is not it?"

"That's all what I know!" The Leader rose from a comfortable chair. "They gave us the coordinates of the location of the base and said that we must survive!"

A strong roar from the outside attracted everyone's attention. People automatically grabbed arms. They left the room and walked along the dark corridors to the exit from the block. Something flashed ahead.

"What is it?" Asked someone.

"Hey, Daphne Collins" came the voice of the Leader. He spoke in a whisper.

"Yes?"

"Do you really see well in the dark?"

"Yes."

"Go near me and..." He screamed before he could finish the sentence. There were shots from all sides. A scream of a creature, probably one that attacked the Leader and screams of people. Monks quickly ran back down the corridor, taking advantage of the turmoil. Their escape did not escape the girl. They fled, grabbing those who were alive.

"Let's run!"

They rushed into the nearest room and closed the metal door behind them.

"Quiet," whispered Johnny. "They can hear us. Or feel."

Behind the door something scraped and made strange sounds. People crouched, holding their weapons at the ready. Johnny surveyed the room: it looks like there were no windows here.

"Hey," he whispered to the girl, "Daphne. You can see well in the dark, as I understand. Look, please, the room."

A few minutes later the girl's voice answered,

"It looks like it's a laboratory."

"Turn on the light," someone said in the dark. "All these creatures know that we are here."

"By the way, they are no longer audible." Another whispered. Then there was a rustle, a curse and a light. The bespectacled stood at the door and was pleased with himself: he turned on the light. People got up. Before them stood a large long table, on which were all kinds of cones: empty and with liquids, microscopes, as well as glass containers with different creatures. At the left wall there was a path anatomical table. People looked at the creatures in the containers.

"I hope it's not the inhabitants of this planet," Johnny said.

"I'm afraid to upset you..." Nestor said, opening a large thick notebook. The survivors stood side by side and looked into this notebook.

"It is doctor Nordock's magazine."

The little fat bespectacled pushed the others and came closer.

"Now, now, now," he whispered, "let me look."

Nestor stepped aside a little.

"And who are you?" The dark-skinned man asked incredulously.

"I am a doctor of Biological Sciences. Oh, oh. Yes, we have big problems," said the bespectacled, looking through a notebook with notes, drawings and photographs.

"This, that plant that devoured the poor creature," Nestor's skin was covered with shivers at the sight of a photograph of a predator plant.

"Right. You have to not approach him more than four meters. Its small shoots - grass blossoms grow just within a radius of three meters: as soon as something alive comes to these blades, whether it is an insect or a larger creature of biological origin, immediately this grass shoots stinging flexible stems..."

"And then it eats," finished tall thin man.

"In general, yes."

"One thing is clear: the rest were devoured by some creature," said one of the men. People dispersed through the laboratory, examining everything that was in it.

"Phew, what an abomination," Johnny snorted contemptuously when he saw the winged dragon-like creature in the container.

"This is also a creature of God. Do not forget that," Nestor said, patting the monk on the shoulder.

"What are we going to do?" The dark-skinned man was worried. "There are only fifteen of us..."

"First of all, we need to examine every inch of this block," Nestor began. "Take everything you need from other blocks and drag them here."

"And how do we do it?" Asked the dark-skinned man.

"What is your name?"

"Mark. Mark Wesley."

"We'll cover each other. We will close the doors of this block."

"We will not be able to hold out here for long." The bespectacled sighed.

People examined the unit for five people. After shooting three fast-moving creatures, Mark Wesley and Steve Moyers reported this to the monks.

"One to the lab, the rest to the scrap," Johnny ordered. "Do you know where the recycling hatch is located?"

"Yes. We saw him."

"Then get these things out of here."

• • • •

PEOPLE GATHERED IN the main building of the administration.

"So, the block is clean. The doors are closed."

"There are almost no provisions here," Daphne said.

"And what did we leave outside?" Asked the bespectacled. Nestor went to the barred window and looked.

"Nothing left."

"We need to examine the other blocks once more, maybe we'll find something," the dark-skinned man suggested.

Six people remained in the main block, in the control building. Among them was Don Hackley, he knew computer technology well. He was left to close and open the doors. And also the monk Nestor and Daphne. The rest checked other blocks and took from there everything that might be useful.

Doctor of Biological Sciences Mattson was in the laboratory and examined the corpse of a representative of this planet, studied the records of doctor Nordock. He was helped by Dr. Richard Haynes. Phil Hartline sat at the table and looked out the window.

"It'll be dark soon," Hartline said thoughtfully, noticing the first signs of dusk. "Where are we going to sleep? I'm tired."

"In the third sector there are rooms for rest for forty people. I saw."

"There were forty of them... All forty people disappeared."

"Stop it, Hartline," Hackley said irritably.

"Yes, you went."

· · · ·

FIVE WALKED IN THE middle, four on the sides of the "five" for cover. They went into the block, inspected, took what they considered necessary, and went out closing behind them the big iron doors. Just in case, suddenly they will have to return to this block one more time. So they checked three backup units. In two boxes they stacked everything they found in the three blocks. The boxes were quite heavy. One box was carried by Jeff Rigwin and Lael Johnson, the second box was carried by David Rothsler, Steve Moyers and Alan Carlisle. In front of the "five" was the monk Johnny, to the left Adam Rutman, to the right of Mark Wesley, and this square chain was closed by Paul McConnell. Nestor looked out the window: the chain of people was heading for the fourth reserve block, looking around and hurrying.

"They entered the fourth block," said the monk, moving away from the window.

"Put the boxes here," Johnny commanded. The boxes were left at the door in the block.

"Rutman, Wesley and McConnell, guard the boxes and the entrance. If that - shoot."

The monk and the others carefully walked along the corridors, looking around and holding the weapon in their hands. They looked around the rooms. After examining the last room, they went back to the exit. Suddenly the light went out.

"Turn on the flashlights!" Said someone. Behind him there was a rustle, and then a clatter of claws on the reinforced concrete floor. Johnny shone where the sound came from. A piercing scream spread through the corridors as the light of the flashlight struck the creature's face. The monk swore and fired.

"Let's run!"

People ran to the exit, some on the road throwing their "trophies."

Creatures slid down the walls and chased people. People saw their glowing eyes in the dark and shot. There was also a desperate struggle at the entrance: three men fired at the same creatures who tried to break into the block through the open door.

Killing all the pursuing creatures, people got to the exit. McConnell shouted: one of the creatures knocked him down with a kick tail and pierced his body in the abdomen a huge claw and dragged the man's body out. Bursting into the unit, almost two-meter creature killed another three people. The outside was almost dark, and they could only see the silhouettes of creatures pounding at the entrance to the block.

"Take boxes!" Shouted the monk. Having won the path, the remaining five moved to the main control unit. Only one flashlight in the hands of the monk, running ahead, shone like a beacon. In the darkness the shots were fired.

• • • •

"THEY'RE A LONG TIME," Nestor said worriedly, and looked out the window. A small light jumped from side to side, moving to the doors of the main block.

"Don! Open the door. Fast!"

Monk Johnny entered last and shot back until the door closed.

"They set us a trap!" Johnny exclaimed, dropping into a chair.

"Close the windows," Nestor said. Hackley pressed the keys and the windows were closed with metal doors.

"These creatures have set us a trap," Johnny repeated.

"I'd like to investigate the corpse of such a creature," Doctor Mattson said holding up index finger.

"When the morning comes, we will try to drag one corpse for you." Nestor looked tired, like the others. "Hackley, did you close the doors well?"

"Yes."

"Then, I think, we will have a peaceful night."

People walked along the corridor to the third sector. Everyone chose a suitable rest room for themselves. Daphne wanted to close the door, but the monk Johnny held her hand. The automatic lock did not work when something was in the way, so the door drove back like an elevator door. Daphne went to the door and stared at the monk. He smiled, leaning, and looked at the girl.

"Do you see through walls? And then my room is opposite." Daphne, smiling cunningly, pushed the monk away from the door and pressed the button. "The door is closed" - informed the computer system when the door merged with the wall.

Hackley made changes in the computer system and now almost everything opens and closes to the voices of people who are now on this base. Outsiders cannot enter or exit - the computer system will not react to someone else's voice. If only... the computer system of the database also issued plastic cards for each member of the team. Such cards were an admission to many areas of this base.

Almost everyone slept soundly that night. Only the monks prayed fervently in their rooms.

In the morning, doctor Mattson was satisfied with the investigation of the new corpse. He found the pages in the journal of doctor Nordock with a description of this creature. Almost two meter creature walked on two legs, like a man.

Outwardly it resembled the ancient inhabitants of the Earth - dinosaurs. The forelimbs were quite long: they reached the hock of the hind legs of five-fingered paws. Brushes of forelimbs had two fingers, at the end of the extremities there was almost a thirty-centimeter claw with jagged edges. Inside the claw, there was a channel through which a deadly poison was produced, produced by the poisonous gland, which is located inside the brush. "Like a snake's poisonous teeth," concluded Mattson. The body was powerful, very reminiscent of the human.

"Which muscles?" The doctor exclaimed admiringly. "If you remove your head, hind legs and tail - a real bodybuilder! It's amazing!"

We must pay tribute to the tail. The tail is very powerful, at the end there is a swept outgrowth. This creature often uses its tail during hunting: with one blow of the tail it knocks down its victim from the legs, breaking the last bone or even killing. It the chest is wide. The head is on a powerful neck and has the shape of a dinosaur's head. Very wide, slightly flattened in the frontal part, jaws broad, elongated, and filled with sharp fang-like teeth in two rows. Teeth are not attached individually, but are part of the jaws. At the edges of the teeth are jagged, like a shark.

"The ideal car is a killer," doctor Mattson concluded. From the lower jaw passes the cervical fold, which connects to the breastbone.

"The only weak point is a delicate thin skin." Said the doctor. "There are no ear holes. It is hunting with echolocation and ultrasound. There are suckers on the limbs. It can climb on walls."

Mattson took the tools.

"Now let's get to the autopsy..." doctor Mattson looked closely and said, "Oh. In the field of the "eye" are special plates - cranial, with a luminous effect."

• • • •

DAPHNE MASTERED A LARGE room in the second sector, reminiscent of the dining room. She tried to cook something edible from what was here and what was brought from other blocks.

During the round table in "management" the question of further action was decided.

"I think it would be nice to establish at least some kind of equipment," suggested Mark Wesley.

"Does anyone know anything about cars?" Nestor asked. Phil Hartline and Wesley raised their hands.

"And me and Johnny," said the monk Nestor.

"Doctor Haynes," Nestor looked at the sturdy, mustached man for forty-nine years.

"Yes," he answered quietly.

"Have you read all the records with doctor Mattson?"

"Yes, I have."

"There are descriptions of any edible plants or..?"

"Yes, there are. Very little."

"Well. We will make transport and we will go to get food."

"If we do..." Johnson muttered.

"So you're in charge now?" Asked the stocky man. His voice felt displeasure. The monks exchanged glances.

"There are no main and subordinates here," Nestor said. "We are one and we must be together. Think and do together. Then we will survive."

"With God's help," he added.

"Among us there are two doctors, a computer technician, mechanics, girl who sees in the dark... And what about the monks sent here?" Asked Wesley.

The monk Johnny turned and looked at the tall man,

"We could pray for you after the death of."

He turned away and headed for the door. All noticeably nervous. Nestor smiled rather, then said,

"It is impossible to establish communication with the Earth. And, it seems, there are no intelligent beings here, except us."

"There are no corpses of that colony either. Maybe they moved to another location," Steve Moyers suggested. He was very young - about twenty. And he was afraid.

"Did they threw all the equipment and left on foot?" Johnson grinned.

"We can only guess what happened here and how. But time is precious."

Nestor left the table and took up his weapons.

"Hartline, Wesley, take your weapons. We'll try to fix something," he said.

• • • •

"WHAT IS IT?" JOHNNY asked. Daphne shuddered in surprise, but did not turn her face to the monk. He stood behind her, approaching her almost closely. The girl felt his breath near the ear.

"I need water. There is only one partial water tank here."

"What else do you have but vision in the dark?"

Daphne turned to face the monk and leaned her back against the table.

"Where are the others?" She asked. Johnny leaned his hands on the edge of the table. They looked at each other searchingly.

"They're waiting for you to feed them, at last," the monk replied with a smile.

"Then call them."

Johnny stared at the girl for a moment, then left.

The dining room was small. It was divided into two halves by a metal table on which food was prepared. In one half stood two long metal tables with chairs on the edges. In the other are kitchen utensils. People sat at the same table opposite each other, but no one took the leading places. Opposite Daphne sat the monk Johnny, next to him was the monk Nestor. Nestor read the prayer, and everyone began to eat. All ate in silence, glancing at each other from time to time.

"It's a pity there's no spaceship here," Alan Carlisle said, breaking the silence, "otherwise we might be out of here."

"If we fix up a car, it's not going to make much of it: the jungle is too thick," Wesley said.

- You'll look for food with your legs, - Johnny said, pointing with your fingers as people walk. Wesley jumped up and spoke threateningly:

"Listen, you... "

Johnny rose from his chair, too.

"Do you want to fight?"

"You are a monk." Lael Johnson began calmly.

"I can forget that." The monk looked at Johnson, then at Wesley. "Before leaving for the monastery, I had problems with the law."

"We both had it," Nestor said. This statement aroused the interest of many present. Wesley could not stand the penetrating gaze of the monk Johnny and sank into a chair. Everyone continued their interrupted meal.

"We lacked only the robbers," growled Johnson.

· · · ·

OF ALL THE EQUIPMENT, it was possible to repair only one Land Rover of old times, using the details of other machines. The men rolled the Land Rover inside the main unit, took the necessary parts and tools, and began to repair.

Daphne stood in the distance and watched the work of four men. The stuffiness made the men to undress to their waists. Compared with others, the monks had athletic bodies. They noticed how Daphne frankly looks at them. The monks leaned over the Land Rover's motor.

"Devil's girl," Johnny heard Nestor swore for the first time in his life on this planet. Johnny smiled and asked,

"It is hard to resist, right?"

"Look how she looks at us."

"It is like she's undressing us," Johnny said, glancing at Daphne. He patted his friend on the shoulder. "Do not forget you are a monk..."

These words Nestor repeatedly told a friend, now Johnny was pleased to say his own words to him.

"Monk, monk..." Nestor grumbled. "First of all, I'm a man."

"Besides, it does not matter here," Nestor added.

"It matters to the Almighty, wherever you are."

Johnny looked up and walked away from Nestor.

Almost the entire seventeen-hour day was spent on the repair of the Land Rover. Outside the windows were darkness, people were sitting in the office.

"Here the night lasts longer than a day, for two hours." Moyers said thoughtfully.

"Tomorrow we will test the Land Rover in real conditions." Wesley was eager to do it quickly.

"We should to split up," Monk Johnny began. His voice was hoarse, but strong and for some reason instilled fear in the people around him.

"Four will go on the car to conquer the local flora and fauna, and to look for something that you can eat. Five will go for a walk on foot. With weapons, of course." Johnny smiled and looked at Hackley and Daphne. "Hackley and the girl will remain here. To guard our fortress."

Daphne jumped up from his chair and was indignant,

"Nothing like that! I'll go with you."

"We can't endanger the girl," insistently said Johnny. Daphne angrily looked at monk rose from his chair. "Then leave Mattson."

"No!" Screamed the bespectacled. "I protest!"

"Hey, you're not in the courtroom," pulling the sleeve of Mattson said Hartline. The fat man sank into his place.

"Then we'll leave the doctor," Wesley suggested.

"No," said Nestor, "the doctor will come with us. We'll send the biologist on the wheelbarrow..."

"That's right," the bespectacled said nodding.

"And her," Hartline nodded towards Daphne, "we'll send her by the land rover."

Some men glittered maliciously in anticipation of the forthcoming trip with the girl. The monks looked at them.

"No," Johnny protested. "She is coming with us."

Nestor nodded,

"Yes."

Don Hackley got up and spoke tiredly,

"Leave Moyers."

He left the table and went to the door.

"Okay," Nestor said. "I, Johnny, Daphne, Haynes and Carlisle will go on foot. Hackley and Moyers will stay here. Others go by the land rover."

Everyone went to bed, having finished the conversation. At the door the monk Nestor stopped the girl,

"I need to talk to you."

"I'm listening."

"Do you understand what you are doing?"

Daphne looked inquiringly at the monk. He stood a meter away from her and looked at her in bewilderment.

"You are bringing trouble to our colony."

"What are you speaking about?"

Nestor stomped on the spot, not knowing how to put it mildly.

"You are one woman among ten men..."

"Eight," the girl clarified, "apart from the two monks." Nestor listened and looked at the door, hoping that no one was listening.

"You forgot," he whispered, "we are not just monks, we're men. And you behave..!"

"And how am I behaving?!"

"I noticed how you looked at us when we were fixing this damn car!" Nestor was angry. He is mad at himself. He approached the girl so close that Daphne smelled his scent, the smell of a man. His lips barely touched her lips. The monk angrily whispered,

"Temptress."

And he hurriedly left the office. Daphne swore and went to her rest room.

Near her door the monk Johnny stood, leaning against the wall and smiling broadly. From his smile it is shivers ran down Daphne's back. The monk held a small wide knife with a curved blade in the form of a hook. With this knife he shaved his head. The girl passed by, trying not to look at the monk, opened the door with an access card and entered.

· · · ·

WITH DAWN EVERYTHING came to life: sounds were heard from everywhere. The colonists took a bite, and then got acquainted with the records of doctor Nordock about edible plant fruits, and only three of them were described, and one animal whose meat could be eaten. This animal was one and a half meters tall and resembled something in between a deer and a cow.

The land rover slowly rode along the soft, silky grass. A light wind blew it. The passengers of the land rover were peering into the grass, holding weapons at the ready. From time to time strange woolly creatures appeared from the grass: small heads with three black bead eyes and a small slit-mouth, a chubby little body with bright orange fur. Small handles were pressed against the breast when these little animals stood on their hind legs. They did not have a tail and ears, but they had an acute sense of smell.

"I wonder if they are edible." Wesley asked.

"I do not know," doctor Mattson answered. "But they are very curious."

The land rover stopped and the hair balls quickly surrounded the car.

"Oh, how pretty," doctor Mattson stammered, and reached out his hand from the open window. Little animals melodiously chirped, ran up close and began to sniff.

Their hair moved, as the emotions they experienced. One hair ball suddenly spat into Dr. Mattson's hand. A sharp pain pierced his hand, and he screamed, sticking it back.

"Little lousy creatures!" Wesley started the engine of the Land Rover and the fur animals were left behind. On the spot spit a gaping wound appeared. Doctor Mattson rubbed his hand against his pants. The pain diminished.

"Bastards! Ugly parasites!" Mattson squealed.

. . . .

ANOTHER GROUP OF PEOPLE was walking as a chain along jungles. Ahead is the monk Nestor, then Daphne, the monk Johnny, Alan Carlisle and Richard Haynes. Thick, outlandish plants made it difficult for people to move. Various voices and rustles rang out above and around them.

"We're being watched," Johnny said quietly, looking around. Behind someone shouted.

The people who walked in front turned: it was Richard Haynes. He did not have a right hand with a revolver, blood rushed from his shoulder. Carlisle wanted to help the doctor, but then from behind the bushes appeared a snake-like head with sharp teeth on the long neck, where there were small a growth - hands. These hands grabbed Richard by the shoulders, and a vile jaw closed on his head. The cry disappeared, as if it were not there. The wrinkled creature, champing and smacking, puffed with pleasure, tearing pieces of flesh.

"Shoot!" Carlisle shouted.

"No," said monk Jonny, intercepting Carlisle's hand with his weapon.

"Take care of cartridges. "

The creature turned his head with his handles and growled. The vile, viscous mucus flowed from his mouth and fell onto the leaves of the plants.

"Let is run!" Shouted Nestor. They ran out into a small clearing, where there was a ten-meter tall tree. Its branches were very thick and were covered with red fruits the size of an apple.

"I hope this is not a tree - a predator," Nestor said, approached the tree and climbed up. The rest followed him.

They sat on branches and peered into the jungle: there was no chase. After carefully examining the fruit, Nestor said,

"In my opinion, it is edible. In the journal of doctor Nordock there was a description of a similar plant."

He tore the fruit off and hesitantly bit off a piece.

"Mmm. Pretty tasty."

"If your feet are not at the level of your head in fifteen minutes, I'll eat that apple, too," monk Johnny quipped. A few minutes later the monk Nestor starts to giggle. Johnny stared blankly at his friend. Nestor laughed. Johnny gaze was clouded.

"What's the matter with him?" Carlisle asked, frightened.

"Maybe this is the agony before death? Alan, what do you think?"

"He-e-he-e-he-e. Hey, Johnny. You have horns," Nestor chuckled, pointing at Johnny.

"Right on his forehead..."

"He was poisoned?" Carlisle was confused. "Before death hallucinations sometimes happen..."

"Do you think it's time for me to pray for his soul already?" They watched for a few more minutes how the monk writhing from laughter.

"You know, it seems to me that these fruits have a narcotic effect on the one who eats them." Supposed to Johnny. "The Lord will not forgive us for this."

Taking a deep breath, Monk Johnny tore the fruit and ate it. A few minutes later they already three of us ate fruits and laughed.

"I think I'm drunk," Carlisle mumbled.

"Good apples," Johnny babbled with emotion. After a while, the hops passed and their mind cleared. They felt full and cheerful.

"We have guests," Carlisle said slowly.

"Oops," Nestor said. A small herd of little animals was approaching the tree, which were described in the journal. They sniffed, chirping. Making sure that they are not in danger, the animals began to eat fruits lying on the ground. A few minutes later, the animals were already lying by the tree, grunting.

"They got drunk," Carlisle said.

"And here are the guests... And where is the girl?" Nestor has thought suddenly. Only now men noticed that the girl were not with them.

Uttering metal grinding, the creatures somehow resembling mantises came close to the tree. They sniffed by their long noses of sleeping little animals, and then by their mantis's feet began to pick up fruits from the earth. In a few minutes even more bizarre creatures joined this "drunken" company. Apparently, among the four groups of creatures present here were both predators and more peace-loving. But they did not touch each other, and now they were all sleeping peacefully together, intoxicated with the fruit.

"While they are asleep, we must leave this place unnoticed," suggested the monk Johnny.

• • • •

DAPHNE DID NOT SEE those who grabbed her. She could not even scream: her voice was paralyzed. The girl tried to escape, but to no avail. Then she fainted. She woke up and opened her eyes. Gently - the blue light blinded her for a while and she closed her eyes. She sat for a few minutes with her eyes closed. Sweetish flavor slowly filled the room in which it was.

The room had no furniture and it seemed there were not even any doors. But the door, nevertheless, was: it opened noiselessly. Daphne felt someone come in, absolutely noiseless and she opened her eyes. She rose to her feet and turned her face to the one behind.

It was a little "man" about a meter high, dark gray-gold color. Short soft wool covered his body. There were four long thin fingers on each hand, three thick fingers on the legs. The small head had a tubular spout, large expressive eyes and small holes - ears. The mouth was not. The girl could not determine sex of this creature. Perhaps they did not have sexual difference, as it was in humans. "I wonder how they say," thought Daphne. "They have no mouth, as such."

The creature melodically chirped, gesturing with handles. Then it approached the girl and touched its hand to her arm. Inside Daphne there was a calm voice: "Sit down." Daphne sat down on the floor. The creature sat opposite and closed its eyes. The girl followed his example. "I'll show you who we are." Color images arose in her head. "We are the Darguns. We live here from the beginning of time. This is our native world. The Darguns lived in harmony with other inhabitants of this planet. Until the Aliens appeared".

"They flew on their supersonic ships," the creature continued. "They call themselves Moruki. The Maruki wanted to enslave us. But we opposed it. Then the Moruki decided to exterminate the Darguns. Only a few could be saved. We hid in the Underground City."

"Moruki conduct experiments, change plants and animals at a genetic level. Some individuals of our planet cannot be changed genetically, or by any other means... But still... it is become more dangerous to live above. Since then we have at war with Moruki". "They are guilty of the disappearance of people who came before you." The creature added. "We managed to save only two: a woman and her child." The pictures stopped flashing in my head, and Daphne opened her eyes.

The little creature approached her and held out its hand to her. "Come, I'll show you the City." They joined hands and the door opened.

Fresh air hit the girl in the face. The combination of various pleasant aromas surprised her. In front of them glimmered an extraordinarily beautiful city, lying in the pit. A myriad of lights sparkled, outlining the buildings of a bizarre shape. Pleasant music came from this City. Wondrous plants grew on the edges and in the middle of the streets. They walked along the narrow streets, and the flowers turned to them. Daphne felt warm and tender, coming from the flowers. Various animals with the riders - Darguns passed them. And no one paid any attention to them. The creatures bowed politely and nodded their heads. Words of admiration stuck inside the girl.

"Where are we going?" Asked the girl. "To people." It was heard in her head. She looked at the little creature: it seemed to her that it was smiling. She understood this on its eyes. And she smiled back. Dargun melodiously, whistling, became to tweet. Surprisingly, Daphne experienced deep respect for these strange little men.

They entered a beautiful corrugated building, built of unknown material. A little man ran up to them, gaily chirping and whistling. He was even smaller than the one who brought her here. "People in the garden. Let's go there." The kid took the girl by the hand and looked into her eyes. She smiled at him affably. He jumped up and cheerfully whistled, and they walked along the long corridor. "His name is Pochi," heard in her head. "His parents were killed by Moruki." The baby squeezed Daphne's hand harder and looked at her sadly. A tear trickled down slowly glass over his fluffy cheek. "Baby." She thought.

The large carved doors opened and they entered the garden. He represented various species of flora and fauna in harmony with each other. The animals of this world were quite inquisitive, but still preferred to be at a respectful distance from an unfamiliar creature - Daphne and watch her from there.

They were approached by a woman and her girl. The woman was about forty years old, long blond hair, slightly curly, felling to her shoulders. She was tall stately, that could not hide under a light, gently-beige tunic. The girl was about seven years old. Large blue eyes gave her look an adult expressiveness, the hair of a sunny color created beautiful curls and was long to the waist. A light dress with cuts on the sides made it easy to move. The woman held her daughter's hand, and looked worried. "We'll leave you," said the voice and two fluffy little men disappeared behind the trees.

"Did they send you for us?"

"No." Daphne shook her head. "We are the second colony."

The woman, silently, stared at Daphne.

"It cannot be..."

"We are in the same situation as you are now."

"They will destroy everybody. Everybody."

"They looked completely harmless!" Cried doctor Mattson.

"You were not liked to them exactly and therefore they spat on you," Johnson growled, bandaging the wound. Monk Johnny stood at the window and looked into the approaching darkness.

"Before I became a monk," Nestor began thoughtfully as he approached Johnny's friend, "I did not care about anyone's life or death. Now, I feel responsible for the life of any creature... But, there are times when we are powerless."

"Yes."

The next day, people continued to explore the surroundings. Now they have changed their modes of travel: monks and Carlisle were go by the Land Rover, Wesley, and Johnson. Hartline and Moyers walked. At the base, Hackley and the wounded Doctor of Biological Sciences Mattson were left again. This time Mattson did not mind at all.

The pedestrian part of the colony slowly made its way through the thickets, cautiously stepping into the velvet grass. Johnson held up his hand. The rest stopped, and then, trying not to make noise they approached Johnson. He nodded to one side. Something black could be seen behind the hanging branches of a liana plant.

"I think it's a cave," Hartline whispered.

"Shall we take a look?" Asked Johnson. They entered the cave. There was absolute darkness in it.

. . . .

LIGHTING THE WAY WITH lanterns found on the base, people moved deeper into the cave. Listening, they walked carefully holding the weapon in their hands. Bones lay on the floor, the smell was not pleasant.

"Ew! Let's go back," Wesley suggested.

"Wait. I see something." Moyers shone a flashlight into the corner. "What is it?"

Three meters from them sat dragon-like creatures. Their eyes were closed, their wings with one finger on the bend and a large claw rested on the sides of the body. Their paws were preloaded under them; the tail with a swept outgrowth lay all the way. Only the crest, which runs along the whole neck and back, then rose, then pressed. It seemed that the animals were dead, but the comb showed the opposite.

"These creatures are similar to those we killed in the main block," Wesley said in a whisper. "They run very fast."

Moyers shone forth.

"There are a lot of them!" He exclaimed.

"Quiet," said Johnson. "We leave. Slow. And do not make noise."

People turned slowly and went. After a few steps, they heard a rustling sound coming from behind. Slowly turning, the colonists saw these creatures which the skin flaking off the body. It was like a butterfly coming out of a chrysalis. Only here the dolls were dragon-like creatures, and butterflies - creatures very similar to those that attacked people in the fourth block: with a huge poisonous claw and teeth in two rows.

"Your mother," Hartline cursed. Someone shouted, "Run!" And all rushed to the exit from the cave. But predators were faster. There was heard the shots, people screaming, the roar of monsters.

. . . .

HACKLEY WAS AN EXCELLENT inventor. In the morning he attached to each suit of the colonists micro sensors, and now it was possible to track the location of each person. These micro-sensors reacted to the heat radiation and vital activity of all human organs, and if one red circle on the display goes off, the sensor host is no longer alive. Now, one after another, four sensors went out. Hackley pushed his feet off the table and carefully followed the display, pressing the keys.

"Something happened?" Mattson asked excitedly, seeing that he was working feverishly with his fingers.

"It seems the hiking men are dead."

The bespectacled rounded his eyes, took off his glasses and nervously began to wipe them. Her hands were shaking, especially the one wounded.

"We're all going to die here. I do not want to die."

"Shut up."

"I do not want to die!" Mattson said plaintively, tapping his glasses.

"Shut up, I said it!"

Monks and Carlisle are still alive.

"We need to take the Land Rover from them..."

"And where are you going by it?" Hackley grinned. He pulled away from the keyboard and leaned back in his chair. After a few minutes, doctor Mattson got up and went to the window.

"What is it?" Asked Mattson. Hackley did not even have time to look at the harmful bespectacled, how there was an explosion. The whole main block was shattered. Just like Hackley and Mattson.

• • • •

CARLISLE LOOKED AT the monk Johnny and smiled. He looked thoughtfully at the land rover's window.

"It is unlikely we'll find her," Alan said, hinting at the monk's sadness about the missing girl. The monk turned his head and looked sternly at Carlisle. The smile slipped from the man's face and, unable to bear the monk's cold look, he turned away. Nestor watched them in the lookout mirror.

Hearing somewhere in the distance the shots and the roar of the collapsed cave, the monk Nestor turned the land rover back to the base. They drove to the clearing on which the base was located and they stopped. Conical ships hovered above the blocks of the base. From one, located the main block, the greenish ray was directed at the block and immediately an explosion occurred. Then explosions of reserve blocks followed.

"It is time to get out of here," Nestor said, and backed up. They tried to slip away unnoticed. But the spy ship had long been following the red pulsating circles on its screen.

· · · ·

THE LAND ROVER DROVE to the open country and stopped. A huge animal was walking in their direction. It looked rather sluggish because of its size: almost four meters high and seven meters long along with its tail. Heavy muzzle, reminiscent of rhinoceros, with small eyes and tubular ears, a thick neck with a longer wool than on other parts of the body, passed smoothly into the withers; a broad, powerful body was supported on four three-toed feet. The tail was an important part for this species of animals: it served to protect against predators and accumulates nutrients and liquid, which allowed these animals to live long without water and food. On his back sat Daphne with a small creature. The animal roared and stopped right in front of the land rover. The men got out of the car.

"We heard explosions. What was it?"

She continued to sit on the back of the animal and looked to the side where explosions came from.

"She did not even say hello," Joni said to himself.

"This base was blown up," Nestor answered.

"It is Moruki."

"Who?" Carlisle asked again.

"Where are the others?"

"They probably died," Johnny answered Daphne.

"Until they found us, follow us."

The animal turned and ran. Dumbfounded by the speed of running, it would seem the hulking behemoth, the men sat to the land rover.

"Not so fast," Nestor said. The land rover barely kept pace with the animal. They drove the long winding and reached the waterfalls. Beautiful waterfalls - big and small - rustled, are creating their own special melody. The animal with the riders approached the rock near the waterfalls.

"Follow us!" Daphne shouted. A small creature whistled like a dolphin and the animal went straight to the rock. The men came out of the land rover, watching them. The air wavered and they disappeared.

"Quickly. Sit down." Said Nestor. The rock was just an illusion. On the other side of the illusion, Daphne was waiting for them, holding a little furry little man by the hand. The animal disappeared into the thickets.

"Leave the Land Rover here," she said as the men got out of the car. They entered the room in which Daphne had already visited. There was a taller man in the room. The little man bowed and sat on the floor.

"Do the same as he does." Daphne sat on the floor with the baby Pochi. The men sank uncertainly to the floor and closed their eyes. What they "showed" were terrible. Carlisle swallowed the sweat. Dargun brought people to the city.

"He leads us to the garden," Daphne said.

"Is he?" Asked the monk Johnny. Daphne ignored his question and continued,

"There are separate rooms in the garden."

"How do you determine where he is, and where is she?" Johnny did not stop. "They're all the same."

Daphne left his question unanswered. The Darguns bowed when people passed them.

"They think we are gods," Carlisle suggested, seeing them bowing.

"No," the girl said irritably. "They welcome us and express respect."

"It's beautiful here," Nestor said, fascinated. The garden was considered the most beautiful place in the Underground City.

"Are we in paradise?" Nestor asked.

"Do not flatter yourself," Johnny said. A woman with a girl approached them.

"Caroline," she said simply, and held out her hand to the monk Nestor.

"Nestor."

The woman shook everyone's hand and introduced her daughter Jenny to them. The woman looked with hope at the men.

A little man of Three Suns took the kid Pochi by the hand, and they left people. Women led the men through the garden, showing them the beauty and splendor of the works of the little Dargun people.

"They have two ships. I saw them." Daphne said.

"Excellent!" Exclaimed Carlisle. "We can now get out of here."

"It's not so easy to do," Caroline said excitedly.

· · · ·

NOT ONLY ANIMALS AND people walked around the garden, but also the Darguns. They collected fruits of trees and berry bushes. When meeting people, they bowed. A little man came out from behind the tree; gray-gold wool with shade immediately struck people. Dargun went to the monk Nestor, holding a basket with pomegranate fruit, similar to a strawberry berry. Submitting the basket of fruit, Dargun chirped and whistled.

"It is Nore. She invites you to try these fruits," Caroline said. Nestor hesitantly reached out to the basket and took one fruit.

"Thank you," he thanked and bit off a little. "Tasty."

Chirped, Nore withdrew.

"You took the fruit from her, and then you are not against her courtship," Caroline said with a smile.

"What?"

"She like you," said Joni, laughing.

"Why did not you warn me?!"

"If you did not accept the gift, you would have offended her greatly. And it's worse than taking courtship," the woman explained.

"And how do you determine where she is, and where is he? " Carlisle asked, looking at Caroline.

"You will live a little among them and begin to discern yourself. It's only at first glance they are the same."

Several separate rooms were located ten meters apart. People stopped near one such room with a carved blue door.

"This is my room," Daphne said. She pointedly entered her abode. Caroline watched Johnny. She very much liked his. The atmosphere of the garden created a special romantic state. Carlisle and Nestor noticed this and left them. Monk Johnny, of course, also felt that this woman was interested in him. He looked at the woman for a long time and then asked:

"Is this yours?" He nodded toward the next door.

"No. My one is that." The woman pointed to the pink door. Johnny, smiling, leaned over and whispered in her ear,

"I am a monk." And he went to the violet door. "I think this one will be mine."

Inside the room, the furniture was not particularly: a lounger on the floor, and on the contrary something like a glass table. There were no windows in the room. The light emitted directly from the walls, which disappeared away if you clap your hands, and it became dark in the room. A few minutes later the door slid into the wall, and the little Pochi entered. Johnny lay on the sunbed, laying his hands under his head. Hearing the man who entered, he sat down.

"What do you want, kid?"

Pochi began to whistle and chirp, waving his hand.

"I see, I see. I must follow you."

He approached and left after Pochi. All the people were led to a small lawn, where there was a low glass round table. They were seated around the table with the three Darguns.

"I am Karagachi. You already know Pochi. And this is my daughter Nore."

Nestor felt uncomfortable and cursed to himself. Nobody began to ask about his wife; everyone understood that she was no more. Karagachi was grateful to them for their understanding.

"I hope you liked the rooms. I think that you will like our food the same way."

On the table there were bowls with fruits, beside each stood bowls with something resembling porridges and lamellar spatulas. People took the wooden spoons and started to eat.

"It's really delicious!" Carlisle exclaimed and noticed that Karagachi smiled. He felt it. Nore did not take her expressive eyes from Nestor. Johnny looked at Nore, then at Nestor, and smiled.

After the dinner, the guests thanked the hosts for their hospitality and went to the rooms. Caroline was walking beside the monk Nestor and talking about something to him. Her little girl was walking beside her. Johnny went to the woman and whispered in her ear,

"He is also a monk."

The woman looked evilly at Johnny, who smiled and went to his room. Daphne noticed this and she did not like it.

Daphne was very sleepy, but she could not fall asleep. To catch up on dream, the girl decided to take a walk in the garden. In the Underworld there are no stars. The light was artificial: there were lantern pillars all over the garden. Daphne walked slowly around the garden, enjoying the silence. She could see Nore coming out of Nestor's room. Then Nestor went out and headed for Johnny's room. A few minutes later Nestor went out and went to his room. Somewhere nearby a beautiful melody sounded, and the girl went to this sound. On the clean platform sat five Darguns and played strange instruments, whistling and chirping.

Seven danced, fancifully moving handles and legs. It was evident that they enjoyed it. Daphne joined them and began to follow their movements. Pochi came up to her and took her hands. He showed her how to move. It was funny, and the girl laughed. The Darguns knew that Daphne could see well in the dark, and so they accepted her as their own.

Opposite stood Johnny, leaning his back on the tree and folded his arms over his chest. He was watching the girl. Daphne noticed him, said something to Pochi and left the site, intending to leave. Johnny barred her way.

"Already leaving?" Without waiting for an answer, he took her hand and led her back to the platform.

"Let's go," Daphne whispered, trying to free herself. But the monk held her tight.

"Hey, guys," he said to the Darguns. "Play this for us."

Johnny sang the melody, not letting go of Daphne. The little men tried to repeat the melody played by the monk, but it did not work out. Johnny sang again and again until he was satisfied with the result. Then he turned to face the girl and took her hand in his, and the other hugged her around the waist. The monk was in a black T-shirt; his muscles were clearly drawn from under it. The fragrance of flowers intoxicated the girl. They danced. Slowly.

The melody, quite, corresponded to the earthly, but still in the manner of the Darguns. "Delightful," - thought Daphne. Johnny looked at her and smiled. She tried to avoid his gaze. Next to him, Daphne seemed very small. She felt uncomfortable.

"Are you afraid of me?"

Daphne glared at him angrily.

"Why should I be afraid of you? You're a monk."

"I can refuse this."

Daphne was silent, turning away from him.

"You're jealous," Johnny suggested.

"Why do you think so?!" Johnny was smiling. Daphne tried to leave, but the monk only held her closer to him. She wanted to slap him, but Johnny grabbed her arm. Daphne raised her other hand. The monk held her hands and smiled. The Darguns stopped playing and squealed, not understanding what was happening between the monk and the girl. Pochi approached them and became interested in looking into Johnny's eyes.

"Go away, kid," Johnny said and turned away from him. Pochi "talked" by ultrasound and Johnny immediately let Daphne go. The kid took the girl by the hand, and they left.

"Oh, my girl was stole," said Johnny frustrated.

The next day, people were shown two ships: one was big, another was smaller. This is all that was preserved after the battle on the surface. Now the best minds of the Darguns were creating a better ship. They were sorely lacking in various details and mechanisms. Before the war, they collected ships at an automated plant in a relatively short time. Now they have to collect manually.

The Darguns decided to help people and gave them a small ship so they could leave this planet. One of the Darguns introduced a flight course into the ship's system, checked the life support system. Telepathically, he instructed people how to operate the ship. At that moment, there was an explosion. The panic began. Inhabitants of the Underground City fled. Karagachi said something to women - the Darguns.

"We need to get out of here!" Carlisle was scared.

"How can you!" Exclaimed Daphne. "We must help them."

"Are you out of your mind?" Carlisle got angry.

"If we do not help them, we cannot get out of here. Moruki will not allow."

"She's right," Monk Johnny said, restrained.

"How did they find..?" Nestor thought. Johnny looked at his friend.

"The sensors," they said in chorus.

"Take off your clothes with the sensors," Daphne said. "They must be destroyed."

"Do you want to see me naked?"

"It is not a joke right now, Johnny."

Karagachi took the children to a safe place, and himself sat down on the big ship with the other Dargun. Small enemy ships were flying around the city and shooting. The Darguns fired back, as they could from the brusik.

• • • •

JOHNNY AND NESTOR BOARDED the ship and took off. The ship with the people swayed from side to side, then twisted in place, demolished several roofs of buildings. Then he leveled and soared skyward.

"Wow!" Nestor exclaimed. The protective layer of the Underground City was broken, so the battle was fought in the sky. The Darguns tried to take Moruki away from the city, where several women were hiding and children. The Moruki guessed this and did not intend to move the battlefield in the sky so quickly. Maneuvering between buildings and trees, a small ship with monks chased the ships of Moruki, and then on the contrary "ran away." Such catch-ups amused the monks.

In the garden, Alan Carlisle shot back how could. He saw only the lights; he did not see Moruki himself. They were hiding behind trees, in the grass, behind buildings. A sharp pain burned his back. Carlisle screamed, and then slowly turned back. For the first time he saw how the Moruki looked: under two, with a small meter, a big ugly head without hair, eyes small narrow, nasal aperture was not, his mouth was without teeth. Instead of teeth there were "brushes" in the upper and lower parts of the mouth, which moved by themselves, two hands with three long thin fingers, one of which was set opposite. Legs are powerful. Moruki could jump well, could cling to a different surface thanks to suction cups on the fingers and change color as chameleons. Carlisle pointed his weapon at Moruki and fired. He did not have time to jump back and fell to the ground squeaking in a nasty voice. Carlisle lay side by side. Someone grabbed Caroline by her hair. She saw Moruki. Screaming in pain and wriggling, the woman dropped her weapon. The creature lifted her by the hair and brought her face close to her. Caroline struck the enemy in the face with a force, he squeaked, and then closed his jaws around her neck. The woman twitched for a few seconds, then died down. The "brushes" did their job: they re-grinded the woman's head like a meat grinder.

Flew over one of the rocks, the monks saw a huge ship. From it flew small ships.

"A ship-womb," Nestor suggested.

"We must destroy it."

They flew to the ship-womb and began to shoot at it. Small lights flashed on the hull of the ship, but nothing changed. Behind them chased Moruki.

"What is this button?" Asked Nestor and pressed it.

"It is ultrasound!" Cried Johnny and they closed their ears with their hands. The ships of the Moruki began to explode. Johnny pressed the same button and everything stopped.

"Johnny, we're falling! Hold control!"

They grabbed the controls' levers of the ship and flew over to look for Karagachi. Finding him, they loomed before his ship. "What happened?" Asked Karagachi telepathically, flying after them.

"Ultrasound disables their ships," Johnny said. "Do you hear us?" "Yes."

"We found the ship-womb. Ultrasound of two ships will not be enough."

"I understood." Karagachi telepathically transmitted to all the Dargunas what to do. The Darguns closed their eyes and began "to talk" by ultrasound. People closed their ears with their hands. The monks turned on the autopilot, and, together with the ship Dargunov, flew to the ship-womb. Ultrasound brought the systems of enemy ships out of action and all the ships began to explode. Moruki could not tolerate the ultrasound. They were rattling and shaking as if it were using an electric current through them. From their eyes, the greenish liquid flowed; it was probably their blood, the scaly skin swelled and burst, after which the Moruki fell dead.

"All the inhabitants of the Planet of Three Suns, thank you for what you did for them," said Karagachi. "You gave us freedom. In addition, you have shown a good way to deal with Moruki." "Everything is ready for your flight," added Karagachi. His hair stirred nervously.

"I'll take the girl with me," Daphne said, pressing Jenny to her side. Pochi approached them and looked Daphne in the eyes. In his expressive eyes, sadness was felt, droplets of crystal tears streamed down the little face of the baby.

"Can I take him with me?"

Karagachi nodded. Pochi happily rushed into the arms of the girl.

"It's time for us," Johnny said. The Darguns bowed the people too. The monks sat in the pilot's seats and turned on the ship's system. The little girl, the girl and the kid Dargun were sitting in the back seats (the children in one armchair).

"The system is ready," Nestor said.

"The flight is set," Johnny said.

"Then go ahead."

The ship turned and took off, disappearing into the silvery clouds.

"Ladies and gentlemen welcome to Earth," Nestor said pleasantly. "Prepare to be planted."

The landing was soft, without shaking. Having muffled the engine, everyone left the ship.

"What the hell?!" Slowly Daphne said. The sky was gray, there was almost no sunlight.

"We landed in the middle of the street," Nestor said. Everything around looked deserted. The wind was blowing. On the right was a rock. Something in it was not so.

"What happened here?" Asked Daphne. Little Pochi tweeted, looking at Daphne, now and then. He took her hand, afraid that she would disappear. Jenny, too, came closer and was press to her.

"There's something wrong here," the monk Nestor viewed the area with apprehension. The deserted street suddenly filled with people. The bulk went to one side. A gypsy girl passed by with a child in her arms, not paying much attention to them, only looking at Dargun.

Daphne and the children went out onto the road. She was asking people what is year now and where is they. But she did not get answers to these questions. Then she turned and looked in the direction people were walking.

"Oh my God," Daphne whispered. The monks looked there, coming to the girl and children. People walked into the city. Urban houses came very close to the village. This street became the outskirts of the city. The people and the Dargun went to the city. On the way they tried to find out from the passing people: what year and what is name of this city. They did not receive satisfactory answers. Daphne was scared. The monks were more reserved. They realized that they were in a completely different time. How many years have passed since they left Earth?

They saw people they knew. Those people looked younger and the changes were noticeable. They walked along the street past the brick abandoned houses.

"I recognize this city and at the same time do not recognize it," Nestor said. Passers-by wore strange clothes, not as they once were.

"Transportation is strange." Johnny spoke for the first time as they returned to Earth.

Ahead they saw a tunnel of red brick and went inside: in the middle are the rails, along the edges are the platform. On these rails went dirty orange transport - something like a train with a bus. Each time a strange semi-bus was swept along the tunnel, people pressed themselves against the wall - the effect of a high-speed train. At the end of the tunnel there were stair leading upward, as from an underground passage. People climbed them and found themselves on the street. Strange cars passed by. Although they did not look weird at all. People passed by. And something in them, in their clothes was not so.

"They hardly get old," Johnny said.

"As if the time for them has almost stopped," Nestor continued. On the right was a tall, beautiful building. People crossed the street and entered this building.

"It is a school," Jenny said excitedly. They walked along narrow corridors. Teachers and pupils passed by. Daphne again tried to find something. But she did not understand them: they spoke indistinctly. Johnny opened the door to the classroom. There at every table sat a teacher, on the table a pile of papers and a computer. To each teacher sat one pupil. There were three or four tables in the class. Daphne opened the door to another class: there - the same thing. One of the pupils looked at Daphne in a way that made Daphne uncomfortable: "Here all girls and almost no boys," she thought. The view of the children was so grown-up... Only now, the girl realized that there are almost no children in the city.

"Excuse me. Where can I apply for information?" She asked the teacher.

"Talk to the secretary," they said. Daphne left Jenny and Pochi to the monks, and she went looking for a secretarial. Entering the secretary's office, and there were three of them, the girl asked,

"What year is it, do you tell me?"

"Two thousand seventy-second," they answered, looking at her in astonishment.

"It cannot be! I need evidence."

One of the women began to pull out from the cells of the locker some papers, notebooks, documents, on which stood the years. She held out one of them, and put the rest back. Daphne looked at the printed inscription in Roman numerals.

"It is two thousand and seventy-two. Cannot be!" Daphne felt not just fear, she felt horror. She left the office.

"Two thousand seventy-two," she said, and took the children by the hand. The monks exchanged glances.

"It cannot be! Say it's a joke," Nestor said.

"If only..."

They left the building and walked down the street.

"Can we go back to them?" Johnny asked, nodding toward the Dargun.

"At first we need to get some fuel somewhere," Nestor answered.

February – March 25, 2006.

"The Devil in the flesh"
"Two Suns"
"When Sphinx will talk"
"The Essence"
"The history of the disappearance of one
the kingdom"
"The Bee Sting"
"The Pet"
Also, for fans of the lyrics, presented a collection of poems
"Beyond the horizon of rains to go."

Contacts

If you have any personal questions or suggestions to the author, please write to e-mail:

kris6778@mail.ru

For business offers:

kris6778@gmail.com

Interview with Kris Solo

What are you working on next?

I am working on a new mystical book " In captivity of dreams".

Who are your favorite authors?

Ray Bradbury, Henry Kuttner, H. G. Wells, Roger Zelazny, Harry Garrison, Stephen King, Clive S. Lewis

What inspires you to get out of bed each day?

My hopes.

When you're not writing, how do you spend your time?

I work, do science, and try to spend more time with my son and my animals.

How do you discover the ebooks you read?

I don't really like e-books. I like to read live books, that is, in print.

Do you remember the first story you ever wrote?

Yes, of course. This was the first fantastic story. I won a prize for it in a creative competition. But due to improper storage by my sister, my manuscripts were lost. Unfortunately, this history cannot be restored.

What are your five favorite books, and why?

"The space trilogy" by Clive Lewis and "The Hogbens" by Henry Kuttner. These books are about me.

What do you read for pleasure?

Science fiction and science books about animals.

What book marketing techniques have been most effective for you?

Recommendations from readers to their friends. I call it word of mouth.

Describe your desk

Computer, sheets for notes and sketches, pen, pencil and eraser. And a calculator.

Where did you grow up, and how did this influence your writing?

I was born and raised in a Siberian village in the Krasnoyarsk territory, Russia. I don't think it influenced my development of the creative personality. You're already born with it.

When did you first start writing?

Since I was six. At this age, I was already reading and writing in block letters.

What's the story behind your latest book?

This is a collection of fantastic stories. In General, it is difficult to call any story the last. Because I write several stories at once. Just some are published earlier, some later.

How has Smashwords contributed to your success?

This is a very convenient platform for publishing books.

What do your fans mean to you?

Fans mean a lot to a writer. If they read my books and they like it, that's good. If the fans took some of my stories for themselves, if my stories made people think about something, then I'm doing everything right and I've achieved what I need.

Does your creativity only show up in writing or something else?

Not only. I draw pictures. In fact, my creativity is revealed in different things. Maybe someday I'll tell you about it.

Don't miss out!

Visit the website below and you can sign up to receive emails whenever Kris Solo publishes a new book. There's no charge and no obligation.

https://books2read.com/r/B-A-ELXT-VIEWC

BOOKS 2 READ

Connecting independent readers to independent writers.

Did you love *Two Suns*? Then you should read *The Aliens Are Steering!*[1] by Kris Solo!

[2]

Two aliens are sent to an unknown planet to study its inhabitants. Their mission did not begin as they expected. Getting into funny situations, the aliens learn a lot about the alien planet and its inhabitants. Follow the adventures of funny aliens, as well as visit distant planets and find out where the Gods are hiding, you can read the stories that are included in this collection.

---

1. https://books2read.com/u/bzre0G

2. https://books2read.com/u/bzre0G

About the Author

Kris Solo is a modern Russian science fiction writer, poet, and painter.

Kris Solo was born on July 6, 1978, in the Siberian village of Pervomaysk, Krasnoyarsk Area, into a family of ordinary workers. Her mother worked in a hard physical job and raised three children alone - her and two sisters. Kris Solo received a veterinary education: in 1998, she graduated from athe Abakan Agricultural College named after N. F. Katanov, receiving a diploma as a veterinary paramedic.

She began writing while still in preschool. She tool part in various creative competitions at school, where she presented her creative works. The first book, "Two Suns", was published in 2015 in the foreign online publication Lulu. Her books soon began to be published in other foreign online publications, as well as in Russian online publication. In 2016, Kris Solo published a collection of poems, " Go Beyond the Horizon of the Rains". Her books have been published in electronic and print form and translared into English.